Bears in the Snow

Shirley Parenteau

illustrated by David Walker

CANDLEWICK PRESS

Here's a bright red sled
on a snowy day.
Where are the bears
to come out and play?

Floppy grabs a cap
to keep warm outside.

Fuzzy pulls on mittens
for a fast sled ride.

OOPS!
Calico's scarf
flies like a kite.

Yellow ties
his boots on tight.

The four small bears
whirl into the snow,
shouting, "Big Brown Bear,
come on, let's go!"

Big Brown Bear
carries the sled.
Four small bears
scamper ahead.

Hmm.

The sled is small.

Just two can go.

First, Floppy zips down
with Calico.

Two more zoom down,
then Big Brown Bear.
It's hard to take turns,
but they want to be fair.

"Let's squeeze close,"
says Calico.
"If we make room,
four bears can go."

They pack together
in a furry ball.
Will that small sled
carry them all?

No!
Yellow falls off
at the top of the hill.
Floppy Bear
is the next to spill.

Then Fuzzy Bear
tumbles into the snow.
Whump! Calico
is the last to go.

Big Bear sees
each little bear fall.
What can they use
to carry them all?

He gets an idea
and suddenly, PLOP!

Big Brown Bear
does a belly flop!

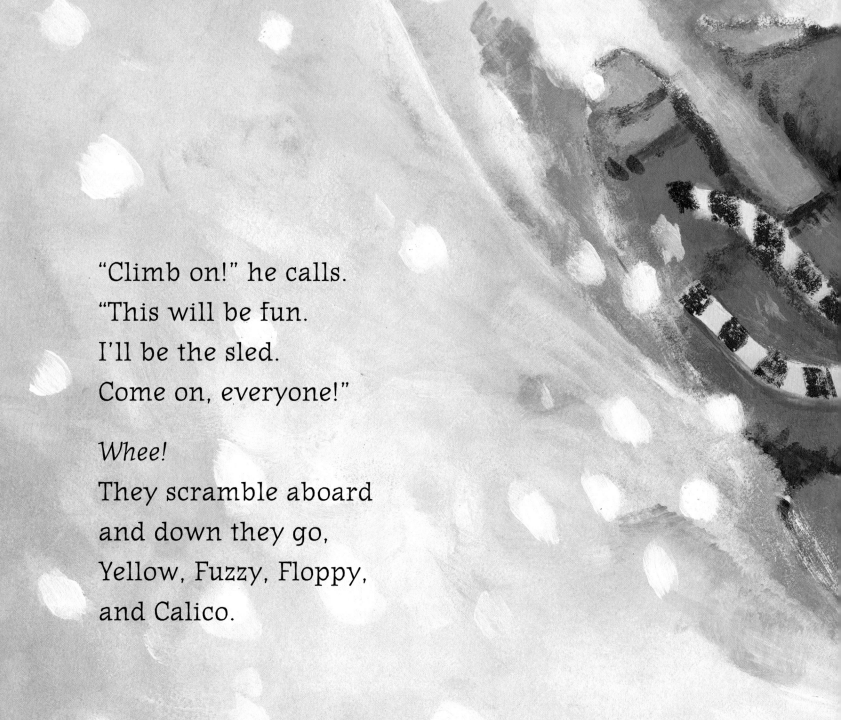

"Climb on!" he calls.
"This will be fun.
I'll be the sled.
Come on, everyone!"

Whee!
They scramble aboard
and down they go,
Yellow, Fuzzy, Floppy,
and Calico.

They shriek with joy.
That hill is steep.
They land at the bottom
in a laughing heap.

More bear sled rides
keep them laughing until—
Is that hot chocolate
they all smell?

Hurray!
Time for hot chocolate!
They run in to share
a warm-up and hugs
with Big Brown Bear.